My Puppy

REISSUED ON THE OCCASION OF
THE 50TH ANNIVERSARY OF LITTLE GOLDEN BOOKS

BY
Patsy Scarry

PICTURES BY
Eloise Wilkin

A GOLDEN BOOK • NEW YORK
Western Publishing Company, Inc.,
Racine, Wisconsin 53404

My puppy thumps his tail when he is happy.
That is why I call him Thumper.
He is thumping and barking to wake me up.

Thumper jumps on my bed and cuddles me.

He wriggles under the blanket and pushes me out of bed.

He shakes my slipper.
He is teasing me.

When I am putting on my clothes I try to dress Thumper, too. He does not like to wear clothes. But he likes to wear funny hats.

At breakfast my puppy wants
a tidbit. He sits up and begs.

When I hold Thumper
up to the mirror he barks
at the puppy he sees there.
The puppy in the mirror
barks, too.

He catches a piece of toast in his mouth.
That is one of his tricks.

My puppy and I like to play in the garden.
There are lots of funny things to do.
We like to slide down the slide together.

Along the border there are flowers to pick. "Hold still, Thumper, while I put a daisy in your collar. Now you are beautiful!"

I am teaching my puppy tricks.

When I throw his rubber ball Thumper chases it and brings it back to me.

He is learning to jump over a stick.

When I stand on my head, my puppy
runs in and out between my feet.

He knows a lot of tricks.
He is a good puppy.

Sometimes he is a naughty puppy.

When he digs for bones in Mother's garden, he is
a naughty puppy.

I must scold him.

I dip his paws into my water bucket to wash the dirt off. And Thumper washes his face with his little wet paws.

Then we play Doctor.
We pretend that my puppy has a sore paw.
I wrap his paw in a bandage.
That makes him feel better.

When the sun is warm,
Thumper and I play in
our wading pool.
We splash
    and kick
        and shout.

After our swim, I sit on the grass in a warm, cuddly towel.

My puppy shakes his fur to get dry.

Thumper likes to play in my sandbox with me.
We build castles and make sand pies.
The sand makes my puppy sneeze.

When I ride my kiddy car,
my puppy barks and chases me.

When I waggle my toy puppy and bark, "Whoof!
Whoof!" Thumper growls and barks.
He likes to make believe. I do, too.

My puppy is sleepy.
He yawns a big yawn.
I yawn a little yawn.
I think it is time for my puppy's nap.
I will have a little nap, too.